The Elves and the Shoemaker

by Mike Brownlow

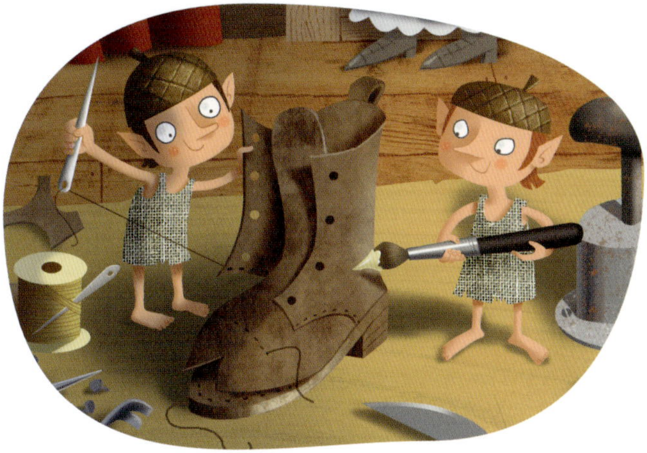

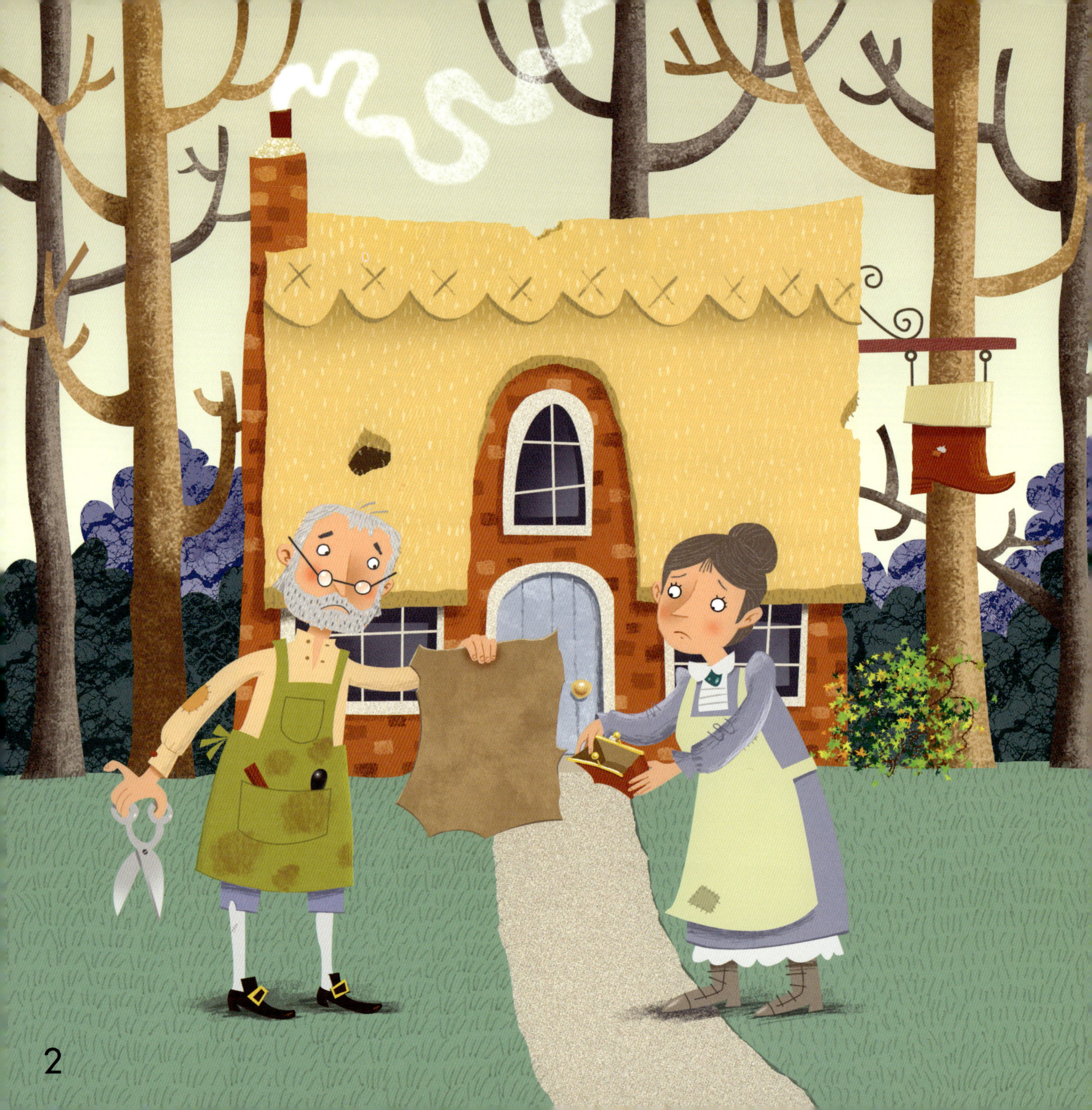

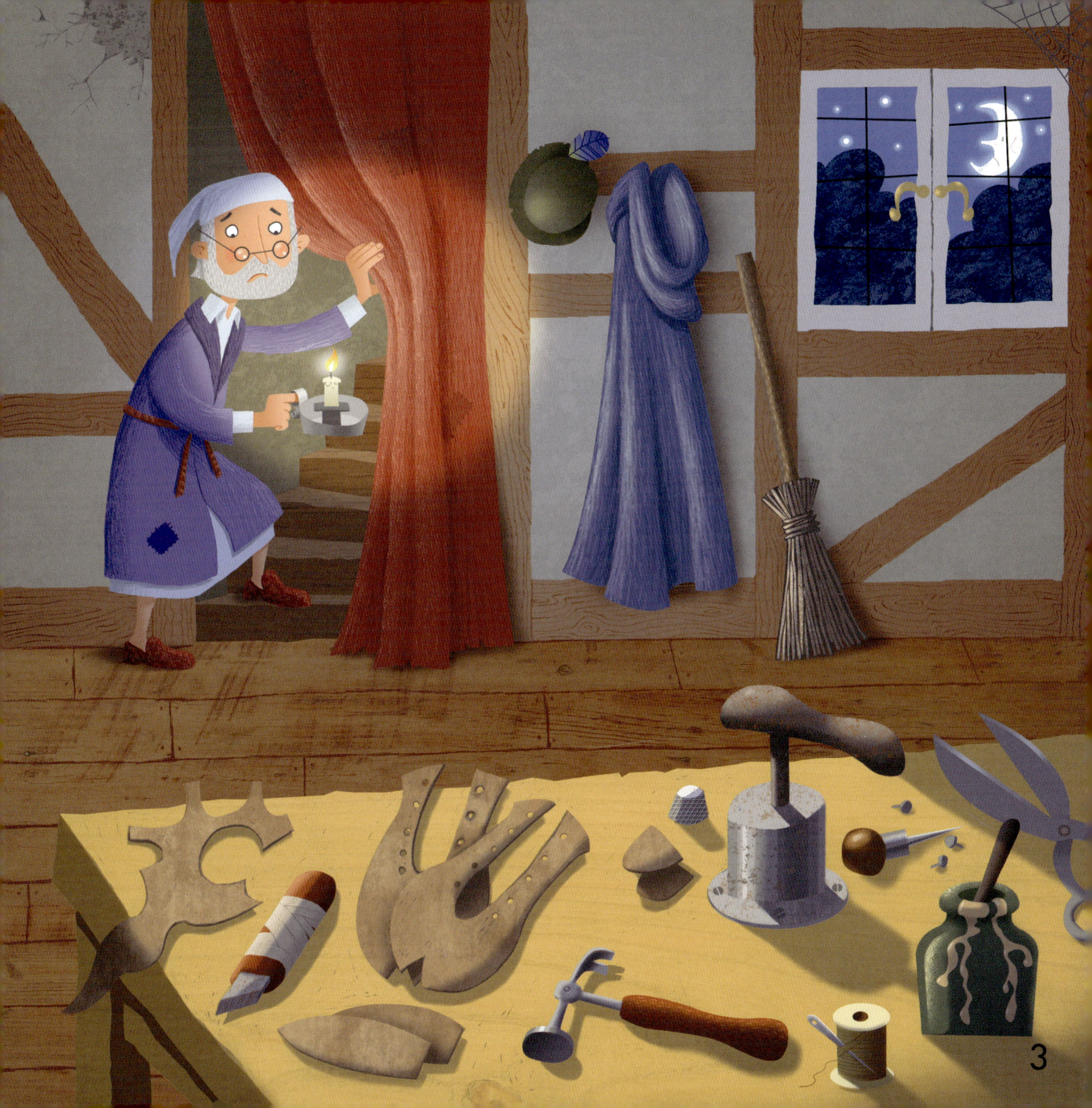

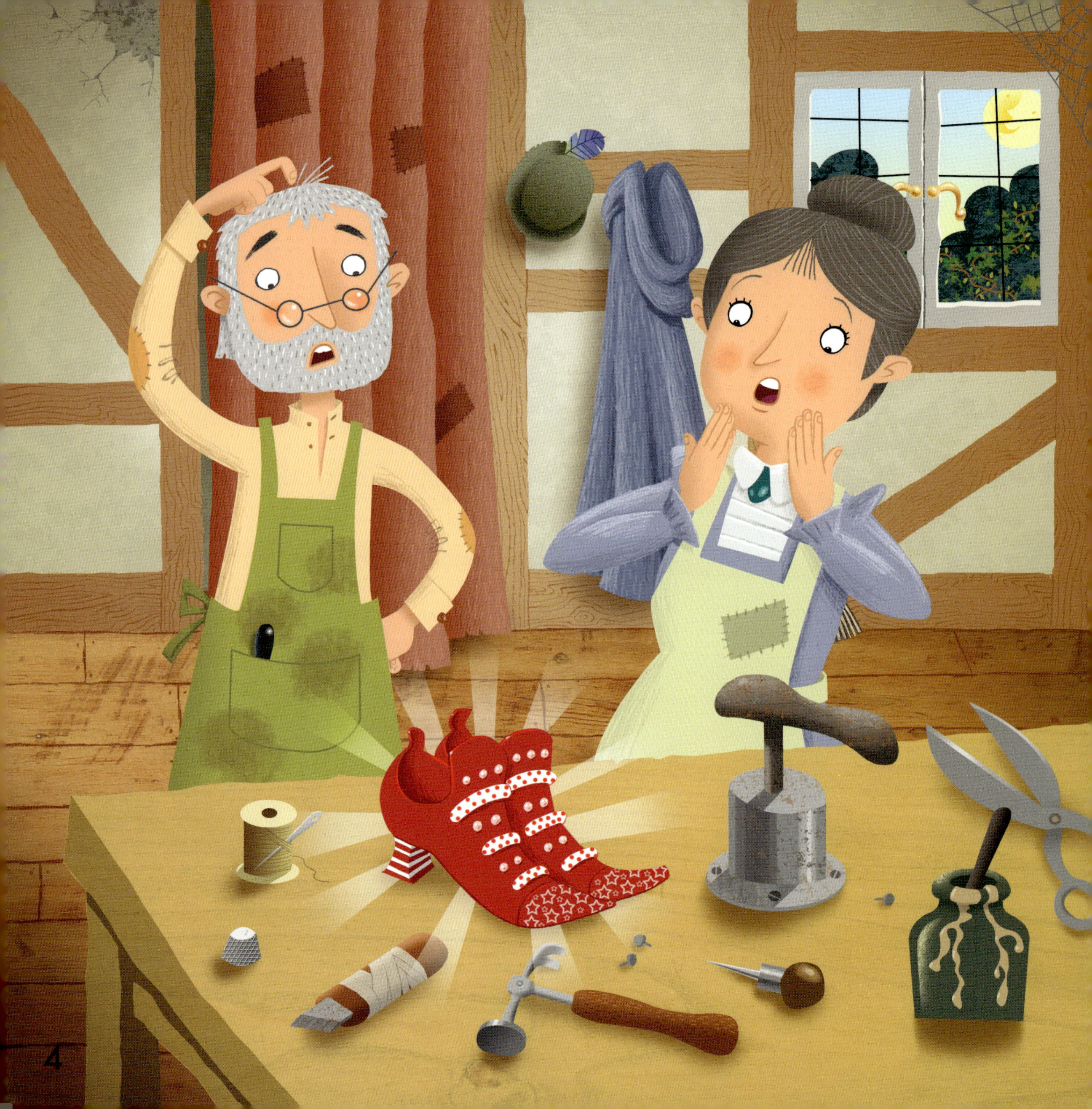

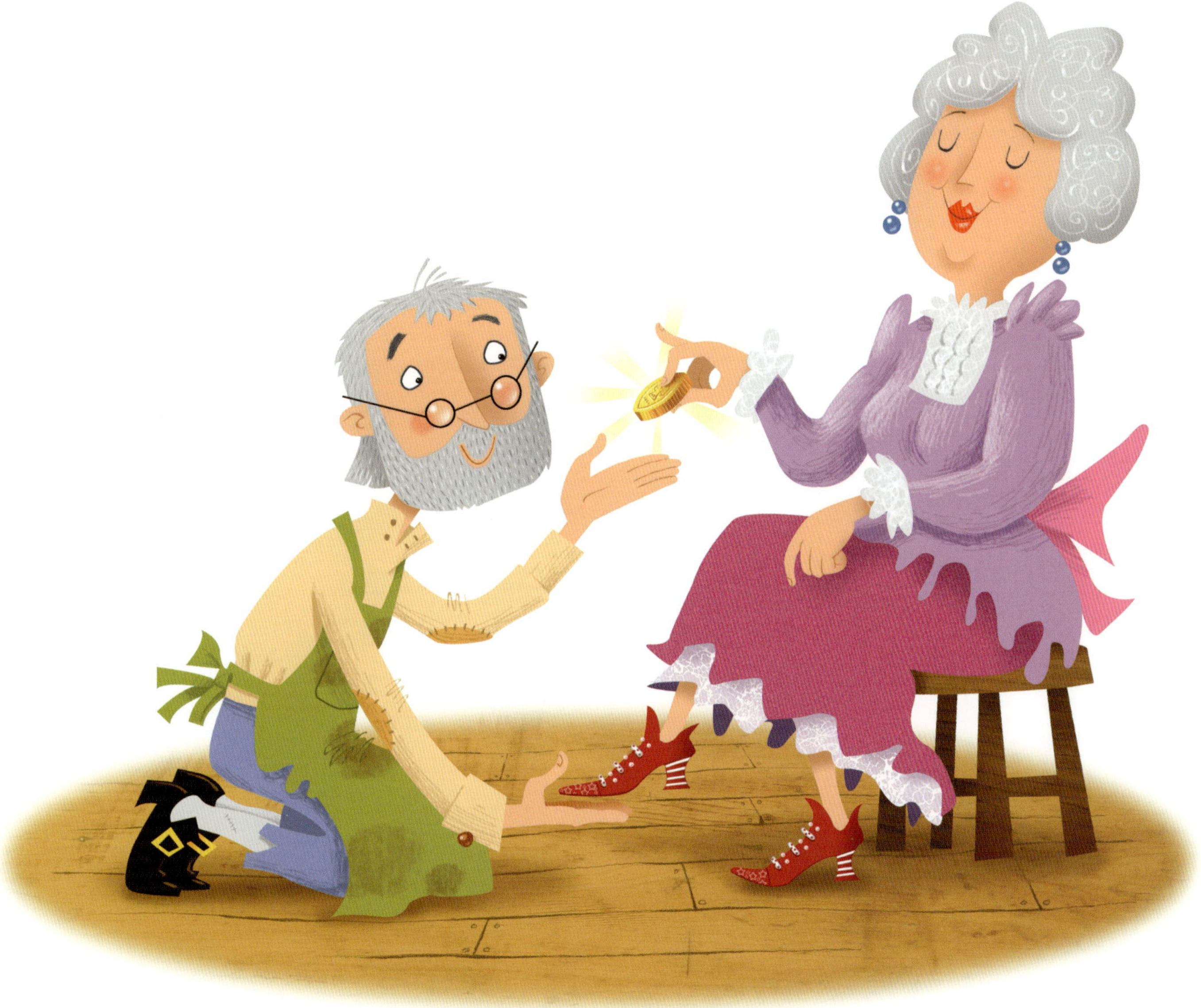

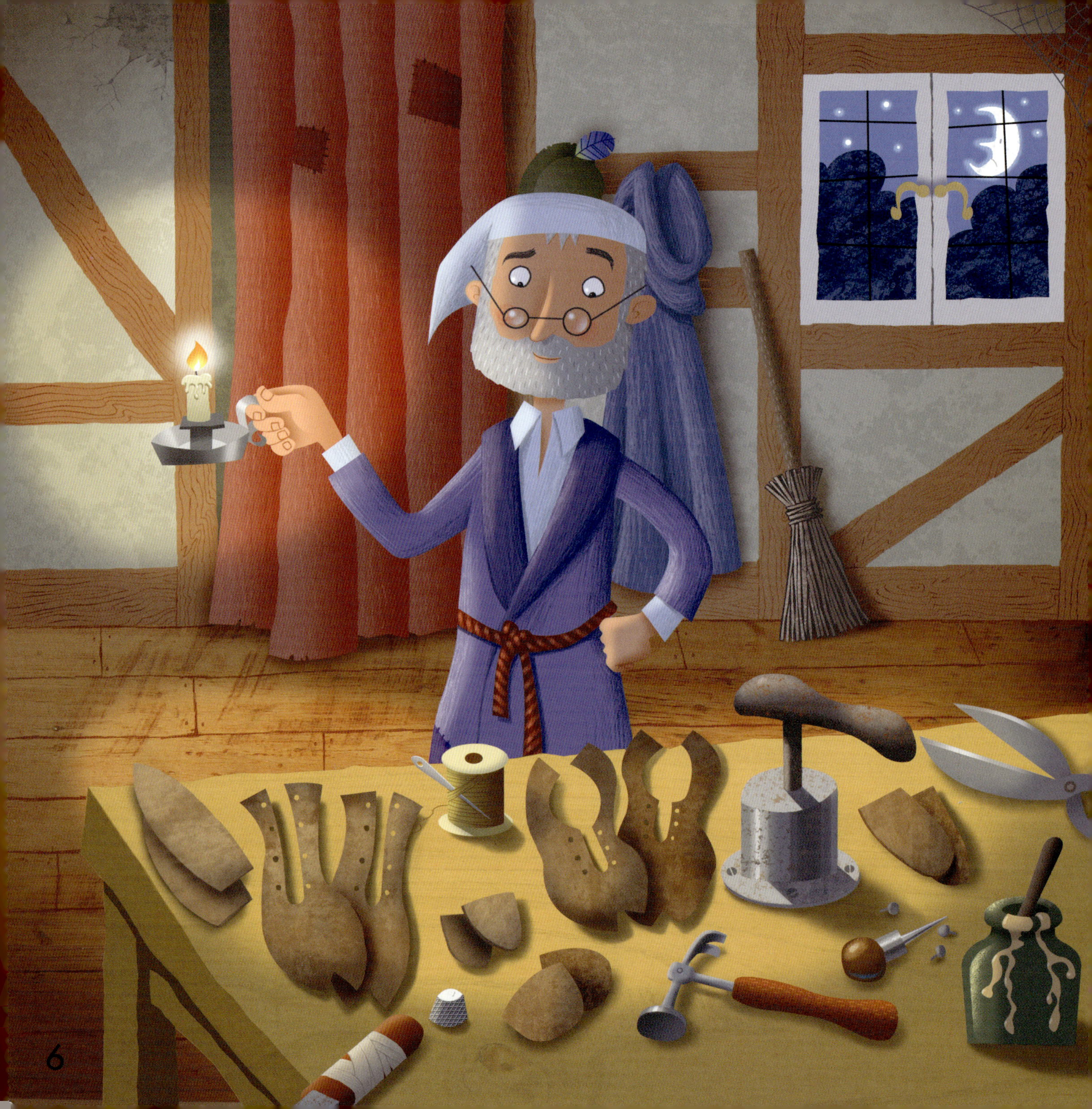

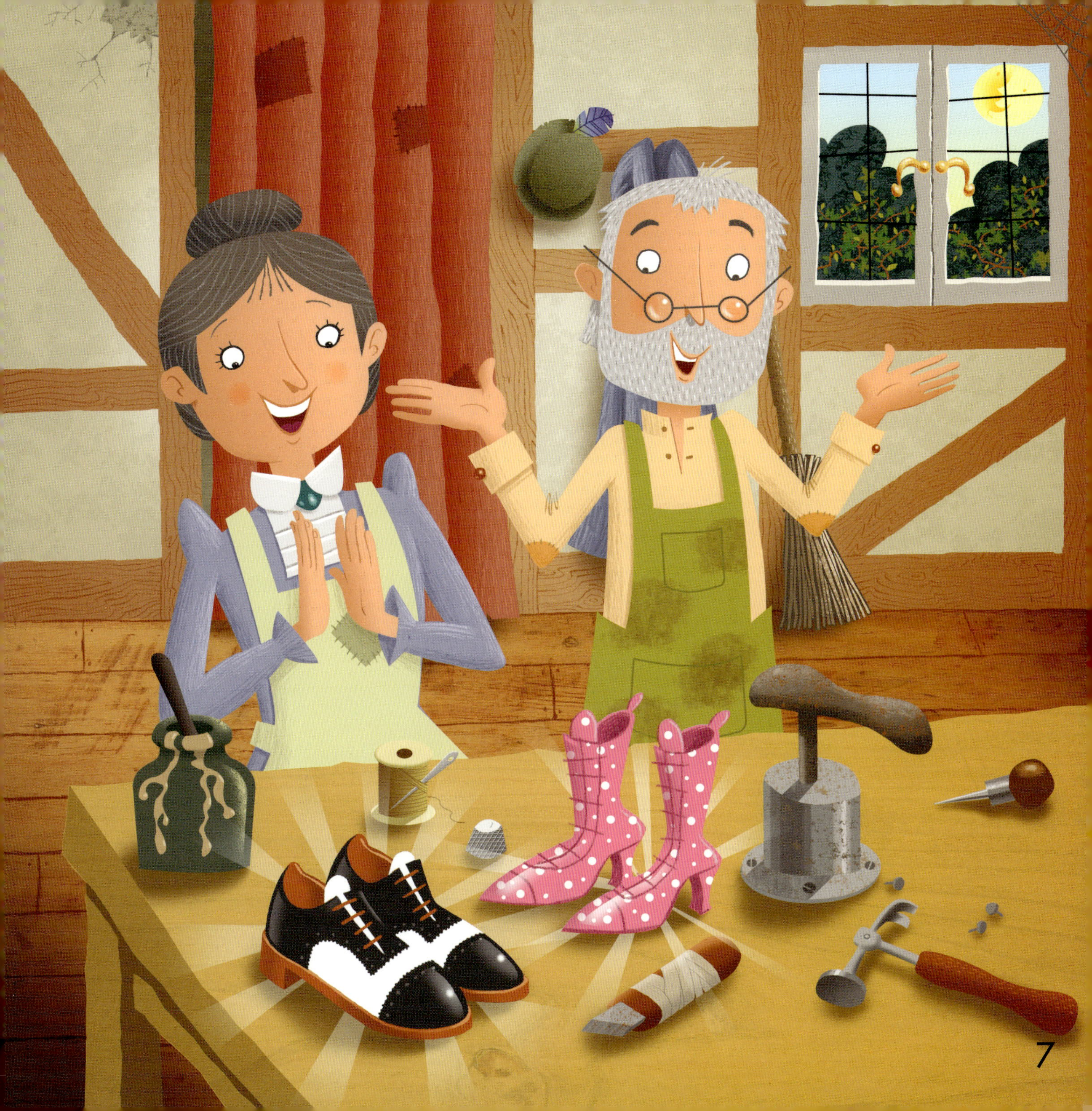

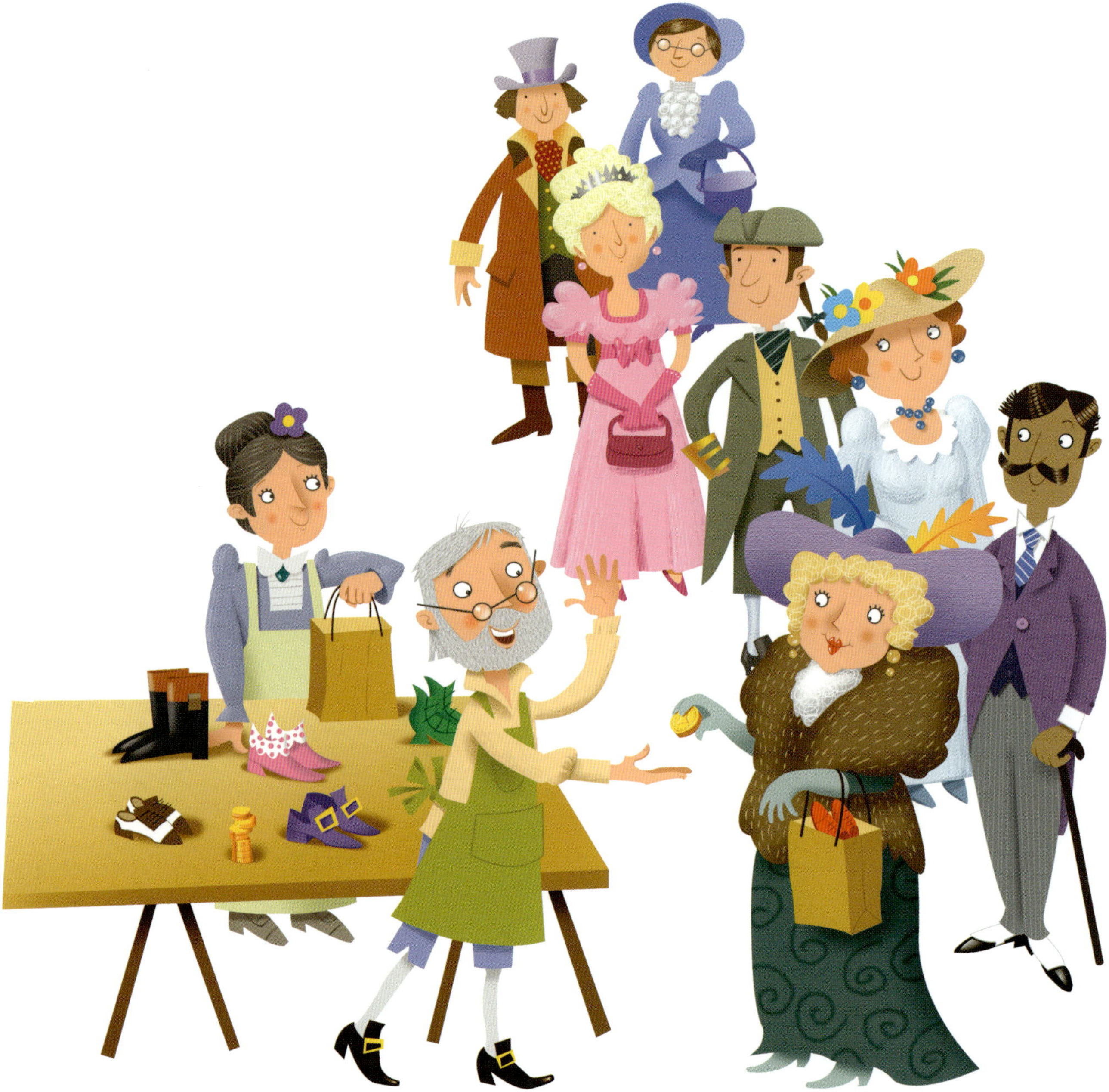

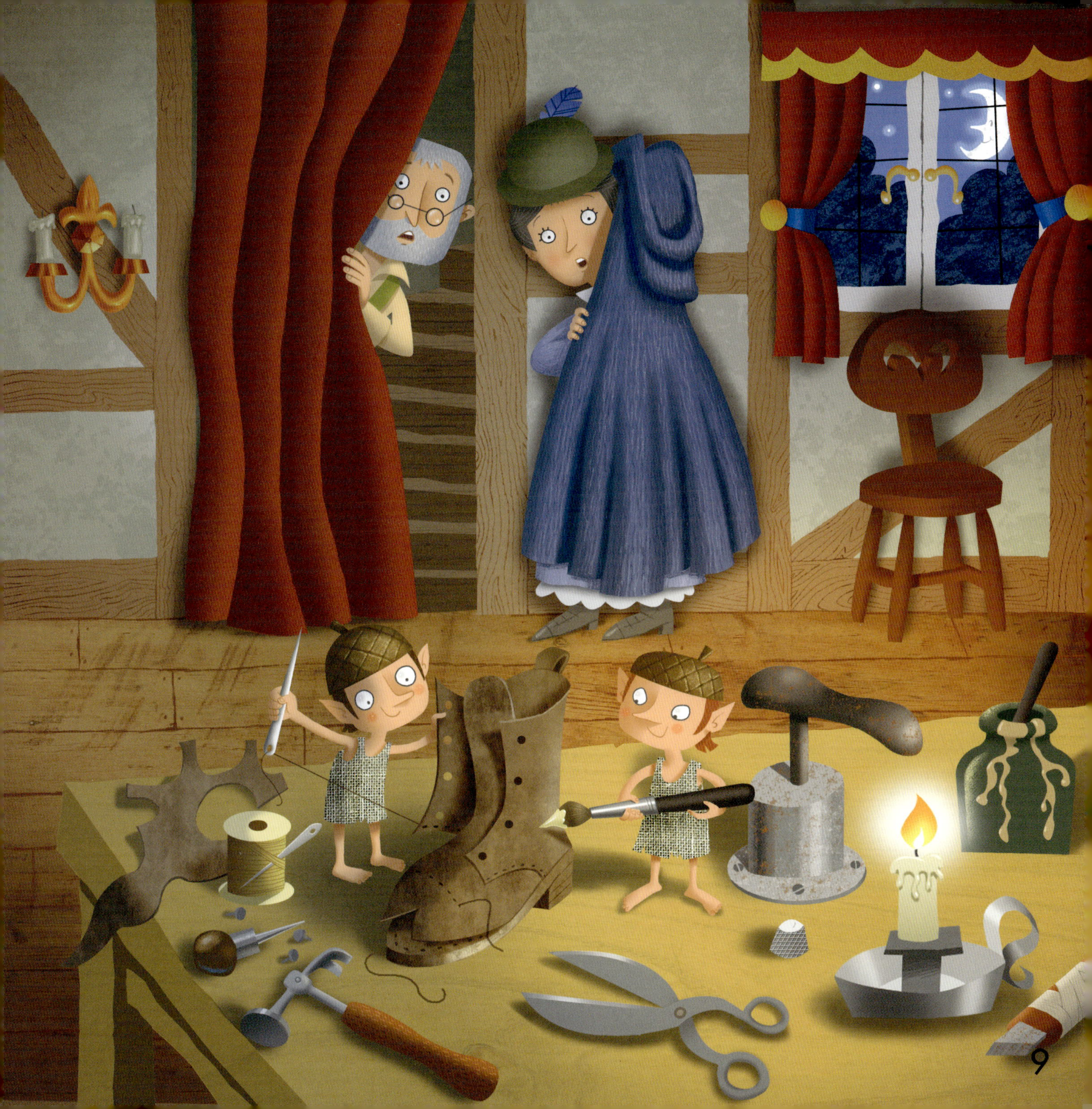

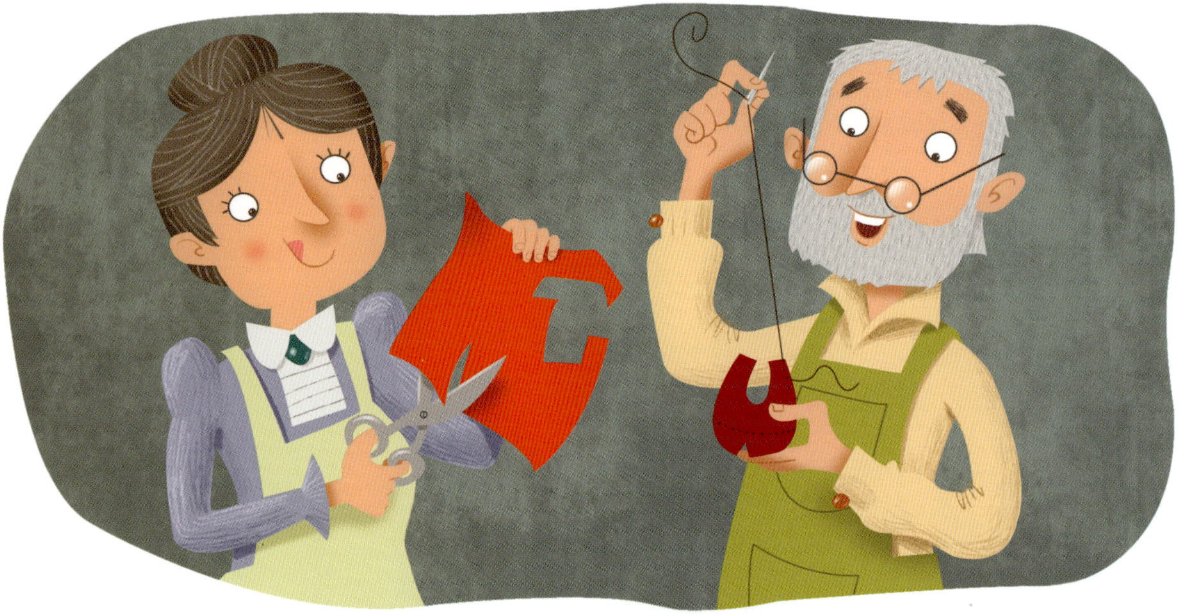

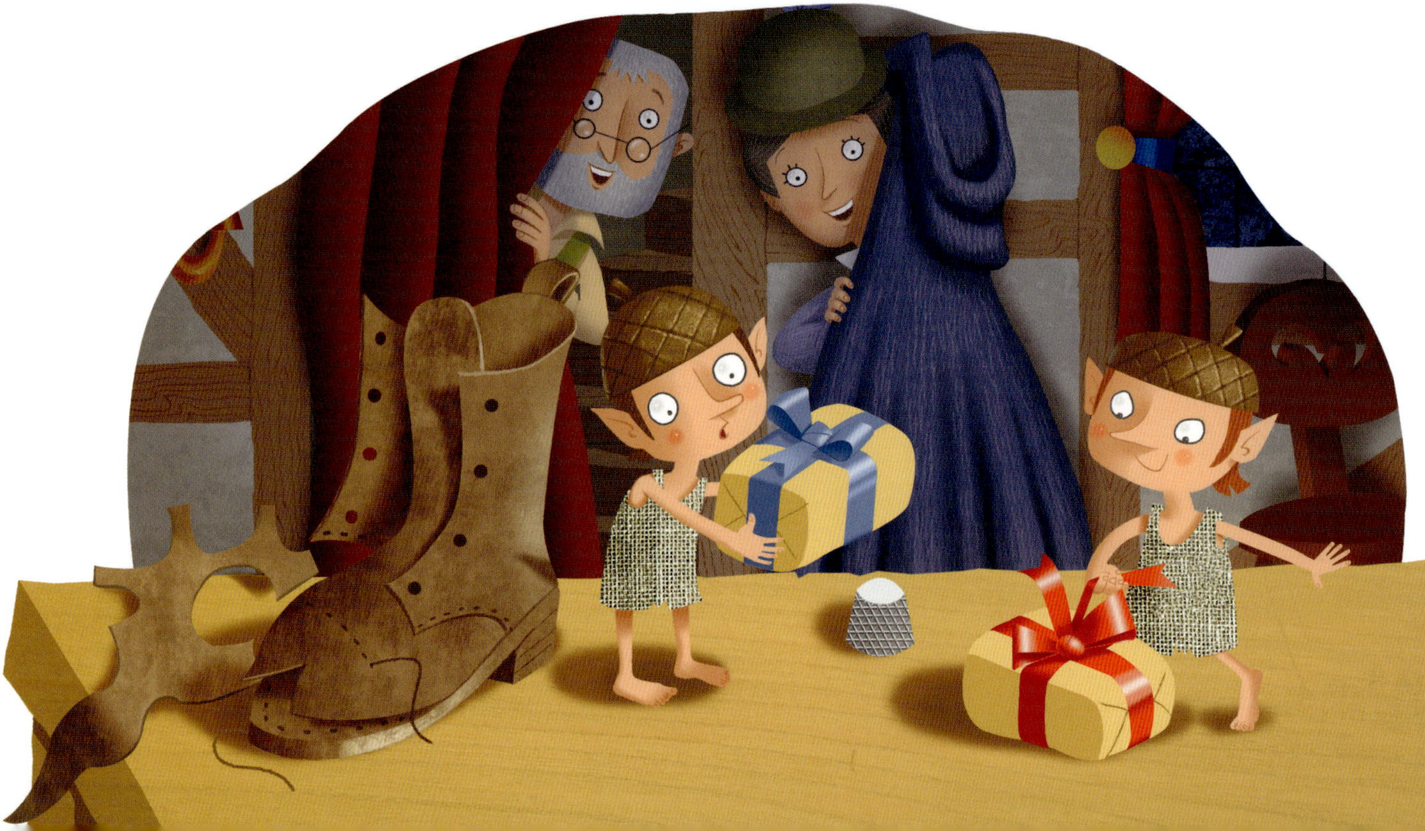

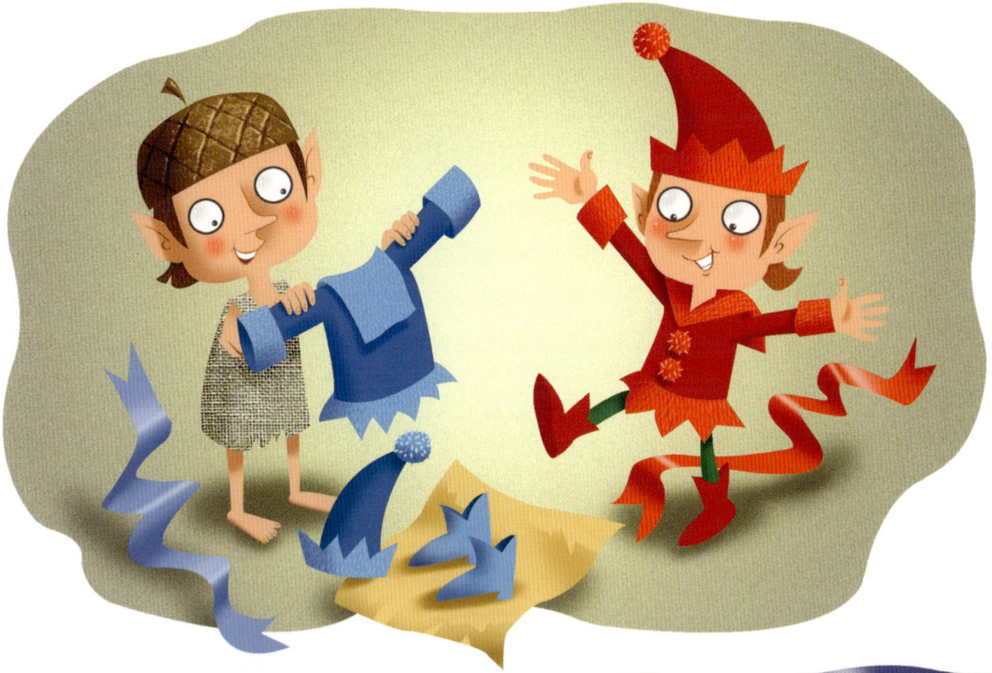

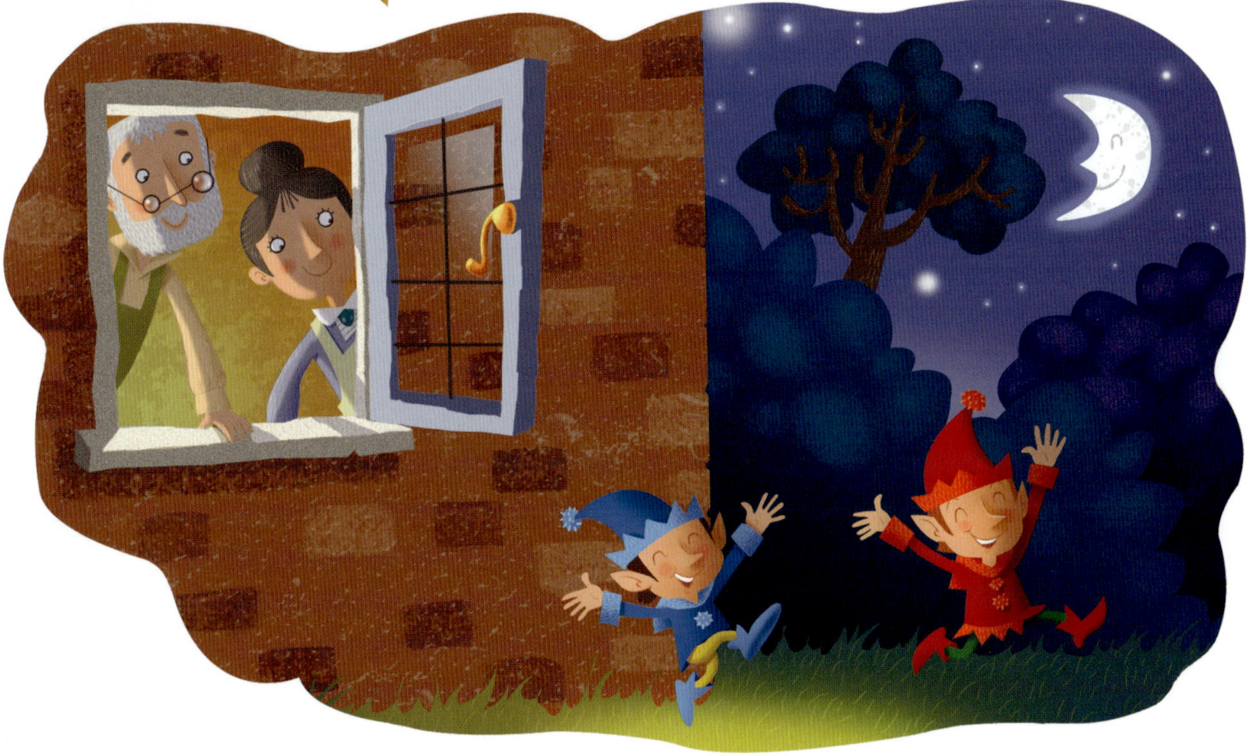

Retell the story

Once upon a time…

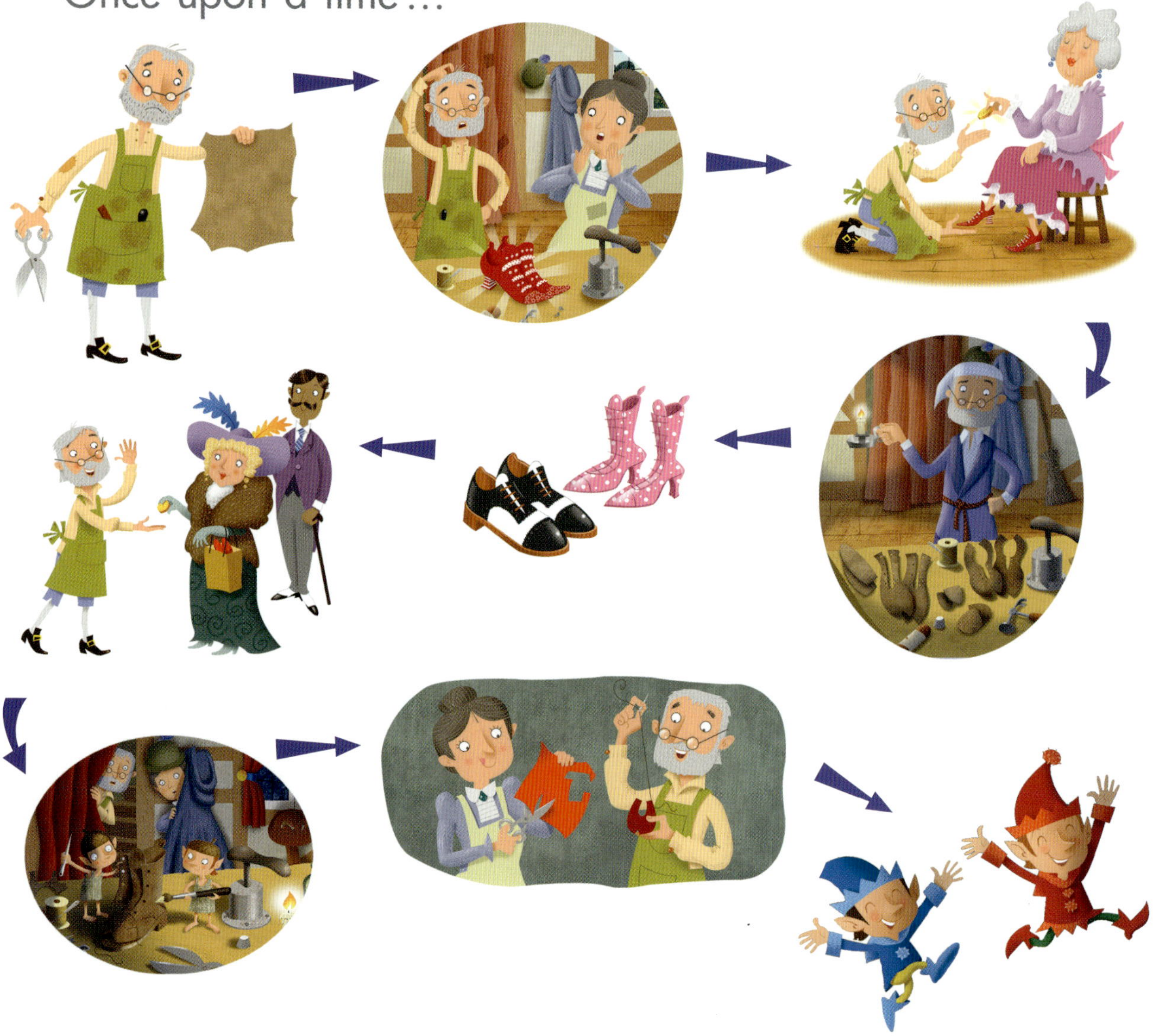

The end.